author of *I Walk With Monsters* and the *Lychford* novels, and writer on *Doctor Who*

"*Shoeshine Boy & Cigarette Girl* is a delightful mashup of all those wonderful old (Depression-era) movies with a tasty SF twist as "moon"-eyed lovers pin their hopes on each other but must deal with a thorough scoundrel first. Enjoy!" — Julie E. Czerneda, author of *Imaginings* and *To Each This World*

"P.A. Cornell is a master of her craft, with a keen eye for the most important things that make us human. Utterly engrossing and imbued with charm, this illustrated novelette of an alternate Toronto is a delight to read. It's bound to put a smile on your face." — Stewart C Baker, author of *The Butterfly Disjunct: And Other Stories*

"Set in a wonderous retrofuturistic Toronto, *Shoeshine Boy & Cigarette Girl* delivers an endearing—and timeless—romantic romp at a time when we need these stories most." — Pedro Iniguez, Bram Stoker and Elgin Award winner, and author of *Echoes and Embers: Speculative Stories*

"*Shoeshine Boy & Cigarette Girl* is a clever modern parable that imagines an alternative Toronto and the dreamers who reside within. Full of deception and resilience, this short tale will leave its readers aching for more." — Nathaniel Luscombe, author of *Moon Soul*

"A pacy and engaging retrofuturistic romp of love, deception, and the power of following your dreams. All the way through, I was hooked by the smooth writing, killer concepts, twists and turns, and the uniquely compelling characters. Highly recommend it!" — Lyndsey Croal, author of *Limelight and Other Stories* and *Dark Crescent*

"P.A. Cornell gives us a fun romantic tale set in a retrofuturistic Toronto. A story not only about fulfilled love but also of trust and care for each other. Shoeshine Boy and Cigarette Girl will leave you smiling and wishing for more happy endings." —Renan Bernardo, Nebula and Ignyte finalist and author of *Disgraced Return of the Kap's Needle*

Shoeshine Boy & Cigarette Girl

P.A. CORNELL

ISBN: 979-8-9914419-8-8 (trade paper)
ISBN: 979-8-9914419-9-5 (ePub)
Library of Congress Catalog Number: 2025950280

First printing edition: February 6, 2025
Published by Stars and Sabers Publishing in the United States of America.
Cover Artwork: Kim Herbst | Cover Design and Layout: Scarlett R. Algee
Interior Illustrations: Ahmed Raafat
Edited by Jendia Gammon and Gareth L. Powell
Proofreading and Interior Layout by Scarlett R. Algee

https://www.starsandsabers.com/

For JP

The Shoeshine Boy to my Cigarette Girl.

Also by P.A. Cornell

Lost Cargo

The Astronaut Among the Flowers

Note

CW: Some language throughout, in particular about/to women, may be offensive to some readers.

Shoeshine Boy
& Cigarette Girl

Visit
TORONTO!
TAXI

Shoeshine Boy and Cigarette Girl first met at Rocket Ray's Diner on the corner of King and Bay, just under the hovercar lanes, in a world very much *like* ours, but not ours. Despite the fact they'd both been raised in this city, an alternate Toronto, their paths might never have crossed had Shoeshine Boy's business not been struggling at his old corner. Tired of competing with machines and making next to nothing, he'd decided to try his luck in the financial district, which happened to be where Cigarette Girl plied her trade. And as fate would have it, on the very day Shoeshine Boy set up shop outside the diner, Cigarette Girl decided to try the place for the first time, treating herself to her usual: coffee, strong, but with lots of cream.

As she approached the diner, Shoeshine Boy noticed her right away. Putting down a newspaper a customer had left behind in which he'd been reading about a police hunt for a thief, he let his gaze settle on her instead. With those cherubic blonde curls and that curvaceous build barely contained by her thin blouse and blue pencil skirt, she reminded him of Lana Monroe, the actress he spent his days daydreaming about to pass the time while shining Oxfords and loafers.

Cigarette Girl hadn't noticed Shoeshine Boy at all. This wasn't because Shoeshine Boy was beneath her notice; she simply happened to be focused on someone else at the time. A guy named Mark. At least that's how she thought of him.

To Cigarette Girl most men were named Mark.

Besides her day job, selling cigarettes to men of means, she had a side gig she'd picked up along the course of her somewhat challenging life. Cigarette Girl was an accomplished pickpocket, you see. She'd taught herself the trade by learning some of the principles of sleight of hand from a magician who occasionally performed at the club where she worked—and whose greatest trick was that he'd managed to bed her once or twice.

Here's how it happened with this particular Mark. As he stepped out of Rocket Ray's, Cigarette Girl spotted the tall, well-dressed man in the fedora. She noticed the quality of the stitching on his pinstriped suit, the silk pocket square and matching tie, the Oxfords Shoeshine Boy had polished to a gleam earlier that morning. She clocked him for a Mark right away, and though she wasn't exactly short on cash that day, she enjoyed a little practice now and then to keep her skills sharp.

The first thing she did was loosen the top button on her blouse in a move designed to look accidental as she brought her hands together to seemingly adjust her wristwatch. This got Mark's attention, and to further misdirect, she gave him a smile—the same smile she used to get the men in the club to choose the imported cigars over the cheaper Luckies and Camels.

"Good morning," Mark said, his gaze dropping briefly to her cleavage as he held the door.

"Such a gentleman," she replied, batting her long lashes as her hand slipped imperceptibly inside his jacket and into the pocket where he kept his wallet. She palmed the leather billfold, ditching it inside her handbag as she continued through the door into the diner. As she ordered her coffee, her hand slipped back inside the handbag and by feel alone she extracted the cash, once again loading the wallet into her palm. She took the coffee, thanking the server with a tip courtesy of Mark, then, while taking a sip from her cup, ditched the wallet into the apron of a passing waitress.

It all happened very quickly and had gone unnoticed by everyone—everyone, that is, but Shoeshine Boy, who'd been watching, marveling at her skill, and who'd followed her inside to see how things played out.

"Nimble fingers," he said, removing his cap as he took the empty stool next to hers at the counter and offered her, of all things, a cigarette from his pack.

"I don't smoke," she told him, which was true.

"This wouldn't be you, would it?" he asked, sliding the folded paper toward her with the article about the thief in view.

She glanced at the words for a moment, then looked him in the eyes.

"That description's so generic, it could be anyone," she told him. "Except they're looking for a man."

"So they are," Shoeshine Boy agreed. "I guess there's no need to call the cops, then."

She couldn't help but smile at that.

Normally Cigarette Girl took little interest in men, besides the Marks. She thought men predictable, and therefore boring. So it surprised her that she found her attention lingering on Shoeshine

Boy. This was clearly not a man of means—obvious from the outfit of cheap brown slacks held up with matching suspenders pulled over a well-worn shirt that had once been white. Not to mention the polish-stained fingernails.

Maybe it was the pleasing timbre of his voice, or his light hazel eyes, or the way his complexion had the same warm hue of strong coffee with lots of cream from which she was currently sipping.

Weeks later she would decide that it was his smile that made her weak in the knees, but it was always more than that with him. Despite his humble position in life, he had an air about him of something more, and she wanted to find out what that *more* was all about.

Shoeshine Boy hadn't set out to move in with Cigarette Girl, so it came as a surprise, though not an unpleasant one, when he realized they'd been living together for over a month. He'd been chipping in for expenses here and there, of course, but nothing official had been said by either of them. With so few worldly possessions to his name, it was entirely by accident that these things had wound up in her apartment over the ensuing weeks. They'd both laughed when he pointed it out to Cigarette Girl, but she hadn't asked him to leave.

They spent days at their respective jobs, looking forward to the quiet moments before dusk when they'd sit on the balcony overlooking the hovercars that crisscrossed over the speedrail track. On clear evenings they could even see the airships docking at the tip of the CN Tower, and they'd tell each other stories about where the ships had come from, or where they might be going next.

But what Cigarette Girl loved best was watching the rockets take off from the island launchpad. Especially when the launch was at night and the moon was full. It was then that she'd tell him about her dream of going there to live in one of the luxury lunar condos.

"I have some cash saved up," she'd say. But then her voice would trail off and Shoeshine Boy knew, without needing to ask, that the money was nowhere near enough, and likely never would be.

"We could always apply for jobs," he suggested one night. "The rich folks up there must need people to shine their shoes and sell them cigarettes, and any number of other things too."

"Sure," she agreed. "I thought of that and put in my application. They've had me on a waiting list for the past three years."

Shoeshine Boy wished more than anything that he'd one day have the means to give her this dream, but he earned even less money than she did, given that he lacked the skill to supplement his income with a little casual theft the way she could.

"What's *your* dream?" she asked one evening, while sipping from her freshly brewed joe with lots of cream.

He laughed. "Until I met you, it was to run away to Hollywood to marry Lana Monroe."

She lowered her cup and gave him a smile. "Silly. Lana Monroe lives in Paris. She barely sets foot in Hollywood if it's not for an award show or big premiere."

"Well, guess it's a good thing I could never afford the airship ticket, then," he said, giving her that smile that caused butterflies to flutter inside her before sipping from his own cup.

"What's your dream *really*, though?" she pressed.

He hesitated for only a moment before removing the wallet from his pocket and opening it to show her a subtle, yet elegant design stitched into the leather. The design resembled a stylized flame, but within this flame she could make out his initials.

"One day I hope to expand my business by not just shining shoes, but also making them," he said. "And not just shoes, but all manner of leather goods, like this wallet. I'll stitch my signature onto everything I make, and people will come to recognize it as a sign of quality."

That's wonderful, thought Cigarette Girl, and in that moment decided that she wanted to see his dream become reality as much as she did her own. He likewise didn't say aloud that these days his dream was simply to see *her* dreams fulfilled. Having never been in love before, they were still new to putting such feelings into words, but they were wise enough to know silence sometimes carried them best.

Wanting to give his girl the moon—literally—Shoeshine Boy began working even longer hours at his trade, so it was early one morning, while most *open* signs, save for Rocket Ray's, remained unlit, that a well-dressed man approached, asking to have his shoes shined. Now most of Shoeshine Boy's clients were well-dressed, but what made The Man stand out was the peculiar way he walked, as though each step pained him.

"Nice wingtips," Shoeshine Boy said, making conversation. "Quality broguing. I don't think I've seen a pair like this before."

"Yes, they're quite handsome," The Man agreed. "Trouble is, I've been breaking these shoes in for weeks and they're still killing my feet."

Shoeshine Boy could see just by The Man's height that the shoes were a size too small, and as he worked, he wondered how a shop that sold such fine footwear could've made such an error. He meant to voice these thoughts aloud, but instead found himself saying, "If you'd like, I could make you a custom pair that'll feel as comfortable as your own skin."

The Man didn't immediately respond, but looked down from his seat at Shoeshine Boy with an expression on his face that said, *tell me more.*

"The price will be more than a shine, of course," Shoeshine Boy continued. "But I'm only just starting to expand my business into shoemaking, so I'll give you a good deal."

The Man seemed hesitant, so Shoeshine Boy kept talking.

"Tell you what, if the shoes I make you aren't the most comfortable pair you've ever owned, I won't even charge you for them," he said. "Just give me a chance, mister."

"This seems awfully important to you," said The Man.

"It is," said Shoeshine Boy. "I've got this girl, see? She wants to move to the lunar condos, but that'll cost more than I make shining shoes, even when combined with her savings and the money she makes selling smokes at The Lone Gander."

"She must be quite a gal for you to go to all this trouble," said The Man.

It was then that Shoeshine Boy reached into his pocket for his wallet, from which he withdrew a photograph of Cigarette Girl, taken on the balcony of their apartment, with rockets launching in the background as the sunset shone golden off her hair.

Upon seeing the picture, The Man let out a low whistle, his eyes lingering on the image of Cigarette Girl perhaps a little too long before handing the photo back to Shoeshine Boy.

"I can see why you're so motivated," he said. "Pretty girl you got there. You're a lucky man."

"That I am," Shoeshine Boy agreed.

"How soon could you get those shoes made?" The Man asked.

"I'll have them ready within a couple of days."

"Well, I *am* eager to get into a pair that doesn't give me blisters. You have a deal."

Shoeshine Boy shook The Man's hand, then set about taking measurements of his feet. They negotiated a price that perhaps favored The Man more than Shoeshine Boy, but he was counting on making up any loss later on, when word-of-mouth attracted more customers. He wasn't normally one to count his chickens before they were hatched, but he couldn't help thinking this was just the beginning and that if all went well, he'd be able to provide Cigarette Girl with the life she'd always dreamed of within a few short years.

It was only hours later that The Man found himself walking through the brass-detailed double doors of The Lone Gander. He'd passed the club many times but had never gone in, having never felt the need to until now.

Stepping through the smoky haze into a room of oxblood silk-covered walls patterned in a damask design, he did not at first see Cigarette Girl standing in a darkened corner by the bar.

Pretending to enjoy the jazz ensemble that entertained the clientele this evening, The Man took a seat at one of the tables, leather creaking beneath him as he settled into the luxurious armchair. For a moment, he perused a menu that listed various libations, but no prices, before laying it back down on the table surface. *If you need to know the price, you can't afford it*, he recalled his haughty stepmother saying on more than one occasion, the thought of that old witch contorting his expression into a scowl.

It was with that very scowl on his face that Cigarette Girl first spotted him. Perhaps it was for this reason that she took an immediate dislike to The Man, though Cigarette Girl liked to think of herself as someone who'd been around the block enough times to trust her gut, and her gut was telling her there was something off about this guy. Regardless, she approached the table. A girl had to make a living, after all, and his money was as good as the next guy's.

"Cigars? Cigarettes?" she asked, using the lively, yet subtly sultry, tone of voice she reserved for customers at the club.

The Man glanced first at the tray of wares she carried, then up along the strap that supported it as it wrapped around the back of her shapely neck. Seeing her now, in the flesh, he decided the photograph he'd seen earlier didn't do her justice. Cigarette Girl was the kind of beauty they wrote songs about. He found himself staring at her heart-shaped lips, her large blue eyes, all the while contemplating how much fun he could have with a girl like that before her looks inevitably faded and he moved on to the next. He stared so long, in fact, that Cigarette Girl was forced to repeat her question.

"Cigars? Cigarettes?"

"Don't mind if I do," he said, selecting one of the thinner, and presumably less expensive, cigars. "What do I owe you, gorgeous?"

Giving him the price, she humored him with a well-rehearsed smile, as she did with all such customers. He made as if to pay her but withdrew the cash just before she could grasp it, instead taking her hand in his free one and gently rubbing her soft skin with his thumb.

"And if I pay a little extra, will that buy me some time in your company?" he asked, thinking he exuded charm.

Cigarette Girl had heard every tired line in the book before, though, and she was unimpressed.

"I'm selling *only* cigars and cigarettes," she told him, her voice now pure business.

Sensing he'd overstepped, The Man now released her hand and gave her the money. In a series of swift and dexterous movements learned under the tutelage of the magician—though she would point out he'd learned a thing or two under her in turn—she took the bills and produced his change, which she placed on the table in front of him.

With that, Cigarette Girl turned to leave. Seeing his chance with her about to evaporate, The Man knew he had to say something to pique her interest before she vanished through the smoke-filled air.

"It's a shame a girl like you is wasting her talents in a place like this. You'd be perfect for the hostess job my friend on Luna's looking to fill."

Despite all her instincts telling her to keep walking, at the mention of the moon, Cigarette Girl couldn't help herself. She stopped in her tracks, turned back to The Man, and found herself asking about the job in question.

"Old college buddy of mine owns a restaurant up on Luna," The Man said, while inwardly congratulating himself on how easily he'd hooked her. "His hostess just quit to start a family or some such. He needs a capable and pretty girl like you to take her place, and just between you and me, he needs her soon."

"Well, that's great," said Cigarette Girl. "As it happens, I'm on the employment waiting list. I'm sure if I'm qualified, they'll notify me so I can set up a video interview."

The Man laughed, pointing to the cigar cutter she wore on a chain at her hip. As she reached across the table to clip his cigar, he explained why he found her statement humorous.

"You'll grow old waiting for a job to come from that list," he told her. "Best way to get a job on the moon is to have an in. As it happens, I'm going to be going up there myself soon, on business of my own. You could come with me on the company dime, as my assistant, and while we're there, I'd be happy to introduce you to my friend."

Despite Cigarette Girl's relative youth, she hadn't survived all this time on her own by trusting random guys. Over her lifetime, plenty of men had promised her the moon—in one way or another—and had invariably left her disappointed. All her instincts screamed at her that this guy was no different. Besides, she had Shoeshine Boy to think of.

Seeing her hesitation, The Man spoke again before she could think too much on it.

"Got a light?"

She reached for a lighter on her tray, flicked it, and held it under the stogie while he puffed a few times until it caught.

"Thanks, sweetheart. Anyway, as I was saying, the best way to get your foot in the door is for my friend to meet you in person. One look at you, and I just know he'll hire you on the spot."

It all sounded too easy, and in Cigarette Girl's estimation, too good to be true.

"Thanks anyway," she said. "But I think I'll stick to the waiting list."

"Suit yourself," he told her, affecting an air of *your loss, honey.* "But I'll leave you my card, in case you change your mind."

He reached into his jacket and produced a plain white business card with his name and business address on it. Cigarette Girl humored him by taking the card and slipping it into the pocket of her pencil skirt, though she had no intention of ever using it.

"Go ahead and take the change too," The Man told her, gesturing toward the money on the table. "You'll need it more than I do."

Two days from their first meeting, Shoeshine Boy was just finishing up a polish on a pair of capped-toe monk straps when he saw The Man again, approaching with a friendly wave right around the time they'd agreed on.

"You're all set," he told the customer in the chair, who promptly paid him before going on his way.

Shoeshine Boy wiped his hands off on a rag to clean the polish off them, then reached into a drawstring bag he'd brought along that morning, producing the brand-new pair of shoes he'd made just as The Man reached him.

"What do you think?" he said, holding the shoes out with pride for The Man to inspect.

Taking a single shoe from Shoeshine Boy, The Man turned it over to scrutinize it, a serious look on his face meant to indicate that he was a person of the highest standards, and one not easily impressed. In truth, The Man knew little about footwear, so while he could see this was a fine pair indeed, the nuance and detail were lost on him.

Consequently, he failed to notice the quality of the workmanship their craftsman had put in. First, Shoeshine Boy had made use of a piece of leather he'd had in his possession for a long time, waiting for just the right opportunity to do it justice. This was not just the softest shoe leather he'd ever come across, but its color was unique: a rich, deep brown, with the most subtle undertone of garnet visible only in a certain light. The style Shoeshine Boy had chosen was a classic wingtip Oxford, perfect for both business and more formal occasions. In keeping with this style, he'd secured the facing beneath the vamp to give the shoes closed lacing. His precise stitching ran in neat double lines along the edges of these, as well as the topline, and in the welt stitching that secured the leather to the best quality soles Shoeshine Boy had ever produced. The shoes were finished with full brogues, running along the curvature of the wingtip shape, along the facing, and toward the heel. And naturally, culminating in a simple design at the toe. They were perhaps as much a work of fine art as they were functional. To Shoeshine Boy, there was only one thing more beautiful than these shoes, and that was Cigarette Girl.

"Not bad," The Man said, as though commenting on fruit just short of peak ripeness, failing to be properly moved by the exquisite object held in his hand. "Of course, I'll need to try them on."

"Yes, of course," said Shoeshine Boy, handing him the other half of the pair.

The Man took a seat on the shining bench and allowed Shoeshine Boy to assist him in removing his old shoes and donning the new ones. Next, he stood, shifting his posture to gauge the shoes' flexibility and comfort. He wiggled his toes, noting the space he now had for such things.

"Go ahead, walk around a little," Shoeshine Boy said.

The Man did as told, unable to hide a satisfied smile as he luxuriated in the comfort of each step. He then paused to inspect the soles, the heel, nodding his approval, though stopping short of saying this was the finest pair of shoes that had ever graced his feet.

"Nice work," he said instead.

Nevertheless, Shoeshine Boy was a receptive man, and so the true sentiment reached him all the same. He beamed with pride at his work, but with all humility said only, "I'm so glad you're pleased."

Then, as The Man walked around a little more, and even performed a few small dance steps—though not good ones—Shoeshine Boy cleared his throat and quietly reminded him that he had yet to pay for the shoes. The price he'd quoted him was barely above the cost of materials, but it was what they'd agreed on, and Shoeshine Boy was a man of his word.

Upon hearing the price, though, The Man scowled, as if he were hearing it for the first time and finding it disproportionate. But then his expression changed to a more congenial one.

"Of course," he said. "You've earned it for this fine work."

He made as if to reach into his jacket for his billfold, then stopped himself.

"That said, I feel as if I'm swindling you, paying so little for your labor."

Shoeshine Boy waved him off. "The price we agreed on suits me fine. If you'd like to help me out more, it would mean the world if you just told your friends about my work, so maybe I could gain a few more customers."

"Sure, sure," said The Man. "That goes without saying. And you can keep my old pair too. They look to be about your size. But I was thinking you could earn some more cash for your trouble. Get yourself and that girl of yours closer to the moon. See, I like you, kid, so I'm gonna make you an offer I wouldn't make just anyone. Tell me something, how much have you earned shining shoes today?"

Shoeshine Boy wasn't sure what The Man was getting at, and silently wondered why he wasn't just paying him for the shoes, but he answered his question, preferring not to upset his first shoemaking customer.

"That's a decent amount," The Man said. "Respectable for a hard-working man like yourself. But what if I told you that you could go home with double that?"

Generally speaking, Shoeshine Boy liked people, and tended toward trusting them more often than not, but, like Cigarette Girl, life had taught him that when things sounded too good to be true, they generally were, so he looked at The Man with some skepticism.

"I've got this friend, see?" The Man continued, oblivious to Shoeshine Boy's expression. "He places bets for me and has a line on a sure thing. Now, if you give me what you made today, I'll hand it over to him. He'll double it, take a small cut, then tomorrow I give you back your money plus your winnings. I won't even take a piece for myself. We'll call it payment for the shoes, plus some extra to take home to your girl."

Shoeshine Boy was hesitant but unsure how to politely decline. He didn't really know The Man well, though he seemed like an upright guy, well-dressed, polite. Still, he didn't like the idea of going home to Cigarette Girl with nothing to show for a whole day's work. What would he tell her?

Sensing reticence, The Man said, "Look, this is a rare opportunity. Like I said, I don't make this kind of offer to just anyone. This thing, it's not what you call above board, if you get my meaning, so we tend to keep it hush-hush, but I trust you. Tell you what, if for some reason this gamble doesn't pay off—which it will—I'll reimburse you for today's earnings, plus the shoes, out of my own pocket. You've got nothing to lose."

Had Cigarette Girl been there to advise him, she would've said that in her experience, strangers didn't do favors for you out of the goodness of their hearts. There always had to be something in it for them, so this overly generous offer would've set off all kinds of alarms for her. But Cigarette Girl was at that moment riding the speedrail home, and up to some morally questionable behavior of her own as she walked along from one car to the next, occasionally poking a set of chopsticks into purses and pockets to see what they might come up with.

"Okay," Shoeshine Boy told The Man. "I'm sure you're good for it."

And with that he handed over his day's earnings to this virtual stranger and watched him walk off down Bay Street in the finest pair of Oxfords in this alternate Toronto.

DINE AT...
ROCKET RAY'S

Cigarette Girl always asked about Shoeshine Boy's day. She didn't specifically mean how much money he'd made; nevertheless, Shoeshine Boy felt it best to steer her away from that before the question even came up. Instead, he told her all about his new customer, and how he'd loved the pair of shoes he'd made for him.

"You finished them already?" she asked. "That was fast. I never even got to see them."

"Sure, but I wanted to impress him. This way he'll tell his friends about me, and I might get more orders. You can see the shoes I'll make for them."

That seemed enough for Cigarette Girl, who went out on the balcony to watch the rockets and airships coming and going, and to dream her own dreams of one day going somewhere too.

Despite affecting a cheerful demeanor when he went to join her, Shoeshine Boy was worried about the choice he'd made to trust The Man. It wasn't like him to get involved in schemes like this, and he was unaccustomed to keeping things from Cigarette Girl. That night, he barely slept, and spent most of the next morning working in silence, too tired to chat with the customers as he normally did.

When he finally saw the familiar sight of The Man walking up the street toward Rocket Ray's, he felt awash with relief. The Man greeted him with a big smile, taking a seat on the shoeshine bench and, once the previous customer was gone, he pulled an envelope from his jacket and handed it to Shoeshine Boy.

"Your winnings, as promised."

Shoeshine Boy had never seen an envelope so thick with bills. He wasn't about to count them right there on the street, but it sure looked like the amount The Man had promised.

"What did I tell you?" said The Man. "Sure thing."

"I don't know how to thank you," Shoeshine Boy told him.

"There's no need. This was me thanking *you* for the shoes, remember?"

"Well, I'm grateful all the same. Maybe I could buy you a coffee in Rocket Ray's or something," he suggested.

The Man laughed. "That's kind of you, but I've got to get back to my place of business. But you know, there's more where that came from and, like I told you, my friend always comes through. In fact, he's got a line on something at the track. Of course, we tend to put a little extra in at the races. A small amount like you gave me yesterday's not worth the risks we take there. And naturally, I'd be taking a small cut myself this time."

Shoeshine Boy, still riding the adrenaline high of receiving the envelope full of cash, couldn't help but be intrigued by this latest opportunity The Man was offering. It sounded like he might need a considerable amount of money this time, though, which was a problem.

"All the money I have is what you just gave me in this envelope," he told The Man, "plus what little I've earned this morning."

The Man nodded and seemed to consider this. "Now, didn't you tell me that girl of yours had some cash squirreled away? You could go home and get it."

"Oh, she'd never agree to letting me gamble her savings," said Shoeshine Boy.

The Man shrugged. "She wouldn't need to know. Just like last time, this is a sure thing. She doesn't count her cash every day, right? She probably won't even have time to miss it before you're back with it and then some. Even if she does notice, she'll be so thrilled she won't care."

Shoeshine Boy did like the idea of being able to surprise Cigarette Girl with a large amount of money, but he couldn't picture himself asking her for her savings, let alone taking them without her knowledge.

Seeing his hesitation, The Man said, "Boy, I wish I had your confidence. A girl like yours has all kinds of options when it comes to men. If I were you, I'd be worried sick I might lose her if I couldn't provide the things she wants. You must be *damn* sure she's crazy about you to go on living day-to-day with just what little you earn here. I envy you."

Shoeshine Boy felt a weight settle into his stomach.

"Tell you what," The Man continued. "Go home and sleep on it. If you decide to go ahead with it, let me know. Bets get placed tomorrow—but no pressure."

He produced a business card from his pocket and slipped it into the envelope of cash Shoeshine Boy was still holding, then walked off, leaving him to his troubled thoughts.

Luckily that didn't last long, because just a second or two later, Shoeshine Boy remembered he was standing there holding a considerable amount of money. So for once in his life, he decided to treat himself by taking the rest of the day off. On his way home, he stopped by a flower shop to buy a bouquet for Cigarette Girl. He chose the most colorful one, which included tulips, lilies, and a handful of Black-eyed Susans. He had the florist wrap it in both pink and violet paper, then tied with a simple white ribbon.

Shoeshine Boy arrived at home just as Cigarette Girl was about to get ready for a late-night shift at the club and surprised her with the flowers. Before she could say anything about the unnecessary expense, he told her that in addition to getting paid for the shoes, he'd made enough money that morning to splurge a little. Then he showed her the envelope.

Cigarette Girl loved Shoeshine Boy for the man he was, and didn't care whether he had money or not, but in spite of all that, she couldn't hide the thrill of seeing all that cash.

"Listen, we've earned a night out on the town," said Shoeshine Boy. "It's not often we have a little extra, so why don't you call in sick to work and we'll go have some fun tonight instead of always doing the responsible thing?"

She thought it over, but the way he was grinning ear-to-ear was just too adorable to argue with. She found herself wrapping both arms around him and planting a big kiss on his mouth.

"I'll go get ready," she then said, and headed back into the bedroom to doll herself up.

Shoeshine Boy loved seeing Cigarette Girl this happy, especially knowing it was because of something he'd done. Still, he couldn't get what The Man had said out of his head. Cigarette Girl *did* have options. He'd often wondered why she'd chosen him when she so often crossed paths with men of greater means, and if he was being honest with himself, he worried she might one day change her mind about that.

It was then that he made up his mind about taking The Man up on his offer to place a large bet for him at the track. The last sure thing had paid off, so this one would too. So, while Cigarette Girl was in the other room, Shoeshine Boy took the coffee can she kept her savings in down from the shelf over the kitchen sink and emptied it of its contents. Yes, it felt wrong, but he knew she'd forgive him when he came back with enough to get them to the moon.

The very next morning—admittedly still a little hungover from the night on the town with Cigarette Girl—Shoeshine Boy took the speedrail to the Distillery District, as per the address on the card The Man had given him. He found himself at an old, rundown building that didn't look like the kind of place where a gentleman might work, but he went in all the same.

Inside, he walked through an empty room in which were stacked several dust-coated cardboard boxes, then down a hallway covered in peeling, faded wallpaper, before coming to a set of concrete stairs. At the top of the stairs he found a non-descript wooden door to which had been affixed a small plaque that bore The Man's name. He knocked once and a moment later a voice from inside the room beckoned him in.

He opened the door on a spacious office with exposed brick walls. In front of the door was an imposing desk, at which The Man was seated. To the right of the desk there was a smaller room closed off by an ornate wrought iron gate through which Shoeshine Boy could see shelves filled with bottles and crates of wine and spirits. Aside from a couple of smaller windows, the room was lit by an enormous skylight of finely crafted stained glass arranged in a botanical design.

"Come in, come in," said The Man, standing and gesturing for Shoeshine Boy to take a seat in one of two green leather chairs that faced the desk. "I'm glad you decided to come down. And perfect timing, as I happen to be between appointments. Even sent the girl out for a break."

Shoeshine Boy hadn't seen any sign that a secretary worked anywhere in the building, but he saw no reason to question what The Man had said. He took a seat in one of the chairs, noticing a small tear in the upholstery, and made a mental note to suggest at some future time that he might repair it.

"Nice place you have here," he told The Man.

"Thanks. Just moved from our old office. Still getting things sorted, as you can see. We're planning on renovating all that stuff out there on the first floor, the hallway and such, to make it more presentable for clients. For now, though, we got this room looking up to spec."

"And just what is it that you do?" Shoeshine Boy asked, realizing just now that over their several conversations, he and The Man had never discussed his profession.

"Oh you know, a little of this, a little of that. Import-export, that sort of thing," The Man said. "I know it's early, but can I get you a drink? Hair of the dog, maybe?" He said this last while taking in Shoeshine Boy's rougher than usual appearance.

"Thanks, but I'll pass."

"Smoke, then?"

"I'm trying to quit for my girl. She hates the smell. Reminds her of the club."

"Sure thing, but let me know if you change your mind. I've got cases of stuff and can definitely spare a bottle or smokes for a friend."

A friend, thought Shoeshine Boy. Was that what they were now?

"So I take it since you're here, it's because you want to take me up on my offer," The Man said, getting right to the point.

Here Shoeshine Boy pulled out a bag from within his coat. The same drawstring bag, in fact, that he'd used to carry the custom Oxfords he'd made for The Man just a few short days ago. Loosening the strings, Shoeshine Boy removed the money. It was all he and Cigarette Girl had in the world. Everything they hadn't spent on rent, or food, or last night on the town.

"That's all I've got," he said, his hand still resting on the pile as if reluctant to leave it.

"That's plenty," said The Man, with a grin. "I'll take good care of it for you. Come back tonight. I should have our winnings by then."

"You're betting some of your own money too?" asked Shoeshine Boy.

"Of course," said The Man. "I know better than to pass on a sure thing. And I can see you do too."

Shoeshine Boy spent the rest of the day feeling uneasy as he distractedly shined Derbys, Oxfords, Chelsea boots, and even a pair of opera pumps later in the evening. The customers he spoke to were all a blur. He didn't even bother to read the papers some of them left behind. He was like one of the shoeshine machines he'd competed with at his old corner, mindlessly and robotically performing the same actions again and again.

Finally, late enough in the day that Cigarette Girl would surely wonder why he wasn't yet home, he found himself again in The Man's office. As usual, he greeted him cordially, but this time added a friendly slap on Shoeshine Boy's back.

"Once again, your trust in me pays off," he said. And with this, The Man produced a sack of his own this time. He placed it on the desk in front of Shoeshine Boy and let him open it. Even with both The Man and his friend each taking a cut, it was more money than Shoeshine Boy had ever seen at one time. A grin spread across his face, at first tentatively, then all at once, until he couldn't help but laugh as he wrapped both arms around The Man, thanking him for everything he'd done.

"Don't mention it," said The Man. "What are friends for? So what do you plan to do with your winnings?"

"Well, you know about my girl, and her dream of moving to the moon," said Shoeshine Boy. "With this, I can finally afford to take her."

The Man nodded, but grew more subdued than he had been.

"What is it?" asked Shoeshine Boy.

"No, nothing," said The Man. "That's great. I'll bet your girl will be happier than she's ever been."

His tone of voice didn't match his words, though, so Shoeshine Boy again asked what was troubling him.

"Look, I don't want to burst your balloon when you're obviously so happy, it's just that you told me your girl wanted to *move* to the moon, not just visit," The Man pointed out. "This'll cover rocket tickets, sure, but then what? You'll get up there and have no way to live. As your friend, my advice would be to let this money ride for a while. Let it grow until you can at least afford to get your shoemaking business up and running up there, and maybe get a small starter place."

What The Man was saying made sense, but Shoeshine Boy wasn't sure about keeping the money with him for so much longer.

Cigarette Girl was bound to notice, and even if she didn't, he hated keeping this from her, and told The Man as much.

"You know how women are," The Man said. "If you tell her, she'll only worry. Just one more bet ought to do it. Better to ask forgiveness than permission, if you ask me."

Shoeshine Boy thought it over. He'd promised Cigarette Girl the moon, after all. What good was it to take her to its doorstep just to give her a front row seat to what she'd be missing? If anything it would be like shining a spotlight on what little he had to offer her and get her thinking she could do better. He couldn't risk that. And hadn't The Man come through already more than once? In the distance he could hear a rocket launching from the island and decided to take it as a sign.

"I'm in," he said. "Let it ride. Plus add in what I made today."

He emptied his pockets and slid the whole lot over toward The Man.

"Wisest choice you could've made."

The minute Shoeshine Boy left his bogus office, The Man separated the real money from the counterfeit bills he'd filled the bag with, smiling to himself over how easily he'd snowed this sucker. That was what he called *his* Marks, and he'd figured Shoeshine Boy for a grade-A sucker the second he'd agreed to let him walk off with a whole day's earnings plus a free pair of shoes.

Here's the way things had gone down after that. The Man had used Shoeshine Boy's money to buy his way into a poker game. Through some skilled cheating, he'd left the game with considerably more than he'd promised Shoeshine Boy and had at first meant to keep it all for himself. But after thinking about it, he'd realized he could take Shoeshine Boy for a lot more money and relieve him of that pretty girl of his, too.

It was then he decided to give Shoeshine Boy the promised winnings in payment for the shoes, as a way to win his trust and convince him to hand over his girl's stash. He could spare a small loss, knowing he'd have more to gain in the future. Just like an investment.

Then, when Shoeshine Boy had let him gamble away both his and his girl's money, there'd been no actual gamble. The Man had used his phony bills to make it seem like he'd placed a bet on his behalf. As for the real money, he'd added it to what he'd kept from the poker game and used it to make a purchase.

It was with this purchase that he arrived at The Lone Gander club, this time walking in confidently and immediately scanning the room for Cigarette Girl. He sat at a table near where she stood, making sure to catch her eye to signal her over.

As she walked toward him, he let his gaze wander freely over her form, taking in each angle and curve, picturing how it would feel to slide his hands over them—and other things too, that are best left in the imaginations of such men.

"My, you are a vision," he told her.

"What'll it be tonight?" she asked coolly. "Cigar or cigarettes?"

"Actually, I have something for you."

With that, he reached into his overcoat pocket and placed two rocket tickets on the table in front of her.

Cigarette Girl studied the tickets in much the same way The Man had studied her. She'd dreamed of going to the moon for so long, she would've spotted a fake ticket a mile away. These she could see were legit. The way the lunar spaceport logo was printed in iridescent ink on the clear plastic surface, the tiny digital speckling that could only be read by the scanners at the launch pad, and of course, the imprint activation sensor located on one of the corners of each ticket.

"One for me, and one for you," The Man said. "All you have to do is press your thumb to the sensor to activate it, and it's three...two...one...blast off."

Cigarette Girl had to admit, she was tempted. Not tempted to go anywhere with this guy, but tempted to steal his tickets. But she had a rule, and that was that the men at the club weren't Marks. She needed this job, and if anything went wrong, she couldn't risk losing both the tickets and her only source of steady income. She didn't like to think about it, but Cigarette Girl had hit some hard times throughout her life—desperate times during which even the most basic of necessities had been tough to come by. She was not eager to repeat the experience.

But nor was she trusting enough to take The Man up on his offer. In the same way that Shoeshine Boy's smile gave her butterflies, there was something about The Man that set her every nerve on edge. *His* smile made her skin crawl. The idea of being up there on the moon with him, depending on him to get back down, was out of the question.

"Look, I appreciate the thought," she told him. "But I just can't take the chance your friend will hire me on the spot, like you say. I have a boyfriend, see? I can't leave him behind not knowing when, or even if, I'll be able to bring him up there with me. And in any case, he has this dream to start a business of his own, making and selling leather goods. I'd rather stay here and help him make his dream a reality."

Cigarette Girl had surprised herself with the truth of her statement. She really was willing to give everything up for Shoeshine Boy, and the thought of him made her smile, and made her a little weak in the knees, as it always did.

The Man misread her smile to mean she might still come around, and so he pushed a little further.

"Don't worry about your fella," he said. "Once you're settled in, it'll be easy to bring him up to join you. Hell, I can even give you a hand processing any necessary paperwork to put the gears in motion right from the get-go. Luna's a perfect place to start a business like that, what with all those people up there, loaded down with dough and so few places in which to spend it."

Being as attractive as she was, Cigarette Girl was used to being underestimated, but she was no dummy, and she knew his offer came with a catch. It didn't take much stretch of the imagination to figure out what that catch might be.

"Thanks, but no thanks, mister. I think I'd rather wait until he and I can both get up there. Now, can I get you a cigar? Or would you prefer cigarettes today?"

It was early on Monday morning that Shoeshine Boy found himself back in The Man's office. Normally this was his busiest time of the week for shining shoes, as most of his customers liked to start the work week with a freshly-polished pair, but he was eager to get the money back—plus extra—from The Man.

"Before we get down to brass tacks," The Man was saying, "let me pour you a drink."

This time he didn't give Shoeshine Boy a chance to decline, which he would've, since it wasn't yet nine in the morning. The whisky bottle and two glasses had already been on The Man's desk when he'd arrived, and now he poured a couple fingers into each glass and handed one to Shoeshine Boy, draining his own glass as he did so.

Shoeshine Boy took this as a good sign that they were celebrating their success, but when The Man put his empty glass back on the desk, his expression was not a joyful one.

"Look kid, I've got some bad news, but I don't want you to panic. I've got everything under control."

Shoeshine Boy had not yet had a chance to sip from his own glass, but sensing that he was not going to be receiving his money as expected, he put the whisky down and waited for The Man to continue.

"Seems there was some kind of misunderstanding between my buddy at the track and one of the jockeys," he said. "A misunderstanding that led to my pal putting our money on the wrong horse. I hate to say it, but the money's gone."

Shoeshine Boy had felt his heart stop only once before, and that had been the first time Cigarette Girl kissed him. On that occasion it had missed but a single beat before resuming its rhythm with the vigorous pounding of a heart in love.

This was not like that.

His heart now pounded so that he could hear it in his ears, tightening his chest so that he could scarcely breathe. It was with great effort that he managed to utter even a few words.

"Gone? All of it?"

"I'm afraid so," said The Man. "But like I said, don't panic. This is just a little hiccup, and I'm gonna make things right. You trust me, don't you?"

Shoeshine Boy didn't know how to respond to that, and in any case, he was still struggling to catch his breath, barely taking in what The Man was telling him as his mind raced with the knowledge of what this meant for him and Cigarette Girl.

"Look, my buddy can be real persuasive when he needs to be," continued The Man. "He assures me the jockey that caused this whole mess will get all our money back, with interest. It's just going to take a bit of time."

"But...I don't have time," said Shoeshine Boy. "What am I gonna tell my girl? She doesn't even know I took the money."

The Man looked genuinely sympathetic—though Shoeshine Boy could not know it was all an act. Had he asked more questions, or even read more of the newspapers his shoeshine customers so often left behind, he would've known there hadn't even been a horse race on that particular weekend. He would've known no bet had been placed. More importantly, he would've known The Man was nothing but a swindler.

"Tell you what," he said. "I'll give you what I've got on me now, just to tide you over. It's not much, but at least you won't go home to your girl empty-handed."

He pulled his billfold from his jacket pocket and handed over a total of forty dollars. Two crisp twenties. Shoeshine Boy, at a loss for what else to do, took the money and placed it inside his own wallet. All he could do now was hope The Man would come through, and that he'd see the money he'd lost again soon.

Cigarette Girl worked late into the evening that day, but knowing he had to come clean to her, Shoeshine Boy had waited up. He worried that when she learned what he'd done, she'd leave him, and at this point he couldn't blame her if she did. Whatever happened, he owed her the truth, if nothing else.

As soon as she came through the door, he rose from the couch where he'd been sitting, walked over, put his arms around her and held her like that for as long as he could before she asked him what was wrong.

"I am so, so sorry," he began. Then he told her everything. He told her about The Man he'd sold the shoes to, and how he'd schemed to get them both money. He told her how, at first, he'd made a good sum, and how all he'd wanted to do was to help her get the life she'd always dreamed of. And finally, he broke the news that every cent they'd ever saved was gone.

Cigarette Girl took all this in without a word. She stayed quiet for such a long time, in fact, that Shoeshine Boy felt the need to break the silence.

"You shouldn't worry, though," he told her. "I'll figure this out. Even if you want to end things with me, I'll see that you're taken care of somehow."

Cigarette Girl was thinking about what this all meant. She didn't want to break things off with Shoeshine Boy, that much she knew. His heart had been in the right place, and it was because he had such a good heart that this had happened. The Man he'd told her about sounded shady to her, but it was just like Shoeshine Boy to trust someone like that. Clearly The Man had played him for a Mark, but he was such a good man he couldn't even see it.

"I'm not leaving you," she told him, and Shoeshine Boy burst into tears. Cigarette Girl put her arms around him. "It's going to be okay. We'll figure something out. I can pick a few pockets. We won't starve, at least."

That much was true, but her greater concern was that rent was due soon, and their landlord was not known for being an understanding man. She wasn't sure they could get enough money to cover that much so soon, which worried her.

"I know rent's due in a couple of weeks," said Shoeshine Boy, as though reading her mind. "We won't be out on the street, though, I promise. I'll work twice as hard—make more shoes. And in the meantime, I know my customer will come through and get us our money back. He just said it would take a little time."

"I don't know," said Cigarette Girl. "How do you know you can trust this guy? You've barely told me anything about him."

"All you need to know is he's a decent guy. He's come through for me before. Look, he even gave me the cash he had on him as a gesture of goodwill."

He pulled out his wallet and handed over the forty dollars. Cigarette Girl took the bills and by feel alone knew them to be counterfeit, but seeing the hope in Shoeshine Boy's pretty hazel eyes, she didn't have the heart to tell him. She knew in that moment they'd likely never see their savings again. Somehow, she still managed a smile.

"That was kind of him," she said. "I'm sure you're right. Maybe I should call on him to thank him. I could give him some coupons for free drinks at the club."

"No, I don't want you having to get involved in all this," said Shoeshine Boy. "I made this mess and I'll handle it. And as soon as we're back on our feet again, I'll go down there to thank him and pay him back every last cent of those forty dollars."

"Alright," said Cigarette Girl. "If you think that's what's best."

Neither of them slept that night, but it was Cigarette Girl who had the most troubling thoughts running through her mind. She'd been on the streets before, as a kid, and had vowed never to return to that state. This was her worst nightmare come true, but she couldn't see a way to fix things.

Save one.

The trouble was, she wasn't thrilled about the option she was considering. She couldn't be sure she wasn't going to land them in deeper trouble than they already were. But she was desperate and could see no other way out.

By the time Shoeshine Boy got up for work the next morning— far earlier than usual—she'd made up her mind. She waited for him to leave, then went to her closet to search her pockets. In one of them, she found what she'd been searching for. She held the plain white business card a moment, considering what she was about to do. But what other choice did she have?

Cigarette Girl took the speedrail to the address in the Distillery District. She reached the building in question just as The Man was arriving for work, so it was that they ran into each other outside. Had she seen the state of the building's interior, she would've known him for a con, but here she saw only a man in a business suit, briefcase in hand and hat on head, on his way back from an appointment, no doubt.

"Well, isn't this a good start to my day," he said upon seeing her. "I'd ask you into my office, but there's dust everywhere. Renovations. You know how it is."

"Of course," she said. "I don't have much time anyway. I'm expected at the club for an early shift. I just wanted to come here to tell you I've thought about your offer, and if it's still on the table, I've decided to take you up on it."

The Man's eyebrows raised slightly in pleased surprise. "I knew you'd come around. Smart as you are beautiful."

She forced a smile in return. "Truth is, I could really use a better-paying job these days. If you still have that ticket, I'll activate it now," she said, wanting to be sure he wouldn't change his mind and decide to bring some other girl along.

"Sure, let me just get it for you." He propped the briefcase up on an old barrel next to the building's door and placed a thumb on the biometric sensor to unlock it. It opened with a pop, and The Man took out a ticket, laying it flat on the surface of the barrel. "Go ahead. Don't be shy."

Placing her thumb on the ticket's sensor, Cigarette Girl pressed down and waited. A moment later, her image appeared, along with her name and other identifying information. The ticket would now only work for her. She was committed.

"Looks like we're all set," The Man said, taking the ticket back and placing it inside his briefcase again before locking it once more. "Rocket leaves tonight. Don't be late."

"I won't. My shift ends early today. Just enough time to go home and pack, then make it to the island with time to spare."

"What about that boyfriend of yours? Did you work everything out with him?" asked The Man.

"I'll call him during my break," she said. "I'll tell him what you said, that if your friend hires me, he can come join me later. That's still the deal, right?"

"Of course. I promised to help you with that, and I'm a man of my word."

"I'm sure you are."

As he turned slightly to grip the briefcase handle, she happened to glance down, noticing his fine shoes for the first time, and the way that in this light the leather seemed to have a subtle undertone of garnet. But more than that, she noticed the stitching along the back of the heel, and how it followed an intricate design that resembled a flame, with initials in it.

Shoeshine Boy's initials.

In that moment Cigarette Girl realized that The Man who'd stolen hers and Shoeshine Boy's savings was the same one she'd met at The Lone Gander. It hit her that he'd played them both, and that even she, of all people, had fallen for it.

She felt the heat of anger rise inside her—*to be taken for a Mark!*

In that same second, she considered confronting him, but she was alone in this place and confronting him now was more likely to get her killed than her money back. So instead, she decided to play along, knowing the moment to act would come soon enough. She smiled as she began to hatch her plan.

The Man, thinking he'd finally won her over, smiled too. As usual, it made her skin crawl, though she hid it well.

A little later that morning, Shoeshine Boy also turned up at The Man's office. Business had been slow that morning, so he'd decided to take a break from shining shoes to come talk to his new friend and see if he might find out when he could expect to see his money again, or at least to ask if The Man had recommended him as a shoemaker to any of his friends. He'd also brought with him his drawstring bag, which contained The Man's old pair of shoes, thinking he might know someone who'd be interested in buying them, since they were still in 'like new' condition.

Had he stayed at his usual corner in front of Rocket Ray's, he would've been surprised with a visit from Cigarette Girl, who'd stopped by to warn him about The Man. Unfortunately, Cigarette Girl had arrived at the corner of King and Bay just as Shoeshine Boy was boarding the speedrail. She'd gone inside the diner to ask after him, but no one there knew where he'd gone. So she'd asked one of the waitresses to tell him she'd come by and to call her at the club as soon as he was back.

After this, she ordered her usual cup of joe with lots of cream, taking it to-go so she could drink it on her way to work.

While Shoeshine Boy and Cigarette Girl were missing each other by mere minutes, The Man was busy planning his exit. He'd emptied out his briefcase and had set the rocket tickets on his desk while he packed all his stolen money into a pouch. He was in the midst of attempting to make the pouch compact enough to conceal under his clothing when there was a knock at the door.

Out of reflex, The Man reached under his desk to grip the handle of a gun he kept hidden there, but when he heard Shoeshine Boy's voice call out to him, he relaxed once more and went to let him in.

"Well, I hadn't expected another visit from you so soon," he said, smiling as Shoeshine Boy entered. "If I'd known you were coming, I would've told you I don't have a lot of time to meet today. I'm off for a few days. Business trip. You know how it is."

As usual he gestured for Shoeshine Boy to take a seat, then headed for the little room where he kept the wine and spirits to retrieve a bottle they might share. Still meaning to return to work, Shoeshine Boy wasn't in much of a mood to drink, and was about to say so when his gaze landed on a familiar face. On the desk, he'd spotted the rocket ticket Cigarette Girl had activated, and at first couldn't understand what he was seeing. Why did The Man have a ticket with his girl's picture on it? And so he stood, taking the ticket and heading over to where The Man was still perusing the bottles.

"What's this?" asked Shoeshine Boy.

"What's that you got there?" asked The Man in return, feigning ignorance. He took the ticket from Shoeshine Boy and inspected it as though seeing it for the first time. At the same time he grabbed a wine bottle at random and started walking back into the office proper.

"Why do you have a ticket to the moon with my girl on it?" asked Shoeshine Boy.

This time The Man turned, swinging the wine bottle at Shoeshine Boy's head, causing him to take a step back. That was enough. The Man shoved Shoeshine Boy the rest of the way into the room with the booze, closed the gate, and turned the key he'd left in the lock. He then held the key in his hand, just out of reach of Shoeshine Boy's grasp, tauntingly.

"Boy, you're not the sharpest tool in the shed," said The Man. "I've met a lot of suckers in my time. *A lot* of suckers. But you, my friend, beat 'em all!"

He walked over to his desk and grabbed the other ticket, shoving them both into the pouch with the money, along with the key to the storage room-turned-prison, then stuffed the whole lot inside his jacket.

"You want to know why I have a ticket with your girl's pretty face on it?" he asked. "Well, that's because when I see something I want, I just take it. I don't sit around waiting for life to do me a solid. I make my own way in this world, and I make it any way I need to."

Here The Man's gaze landed on a newspaper clipping from a while back that he'd held onto as a kind of souvenir. But now, it gave him an idea.

The clipping, as it happened, was from the very newspaper Shoeshine Boy had been reading when he and Cigarette Girl had first met. In fact, it was the very article he'd shown her that included a description of a thief the police had been hunting. The Man took the clipping and read this description aloud to Shoeshine Boy.

"Let's see...suspect is male, approximately six feet in height." He paused to measure Shoeshine Boy with his eyes. "Close enough. What else? Short dark hair. Check. Well-dressed, okay, maybe not quite that one, but it's been a while, a man can always fall on hard times, right?"

He went on like this, listing all the qualities witnesses had provided, and Shoeshine Boy could see what he was getting at. Cigarette Girl had said the description was so generic, it could fit just about anyone, and so it was that Shoeshine Boy could see how under the right circumstances, even he could be mistaken for the thief. He could also see that The Man fit the description to a T, and now he understood that it was *he* the police were no doubt still looking for. How many people had he stolen from before finding his way to Shoeshine Boy at the corner of King and Bay? How many crimes had he already gotten away with? And now, he'd somehow managed to get Cigarette Girl too. He couldn't let this happen.

Shoeshine Boy threw his weight against the gated door to the little storage room, but the hinges were surprisingly strong. Again and again he pushed and pulled, but the gate wouldn't budge.

"Rattle your cage all you want," The Man said. "You're not going anywhere until the cops come for you—after I've tipped them off, being the concerned citizen that I am."

"It'll never work," said Shoeshine Boy. "They'll figure out I'm not the thief in no time. There's no way I'll take the fall for you."

"I'm sure you're right," said The Man. "But by the time they sort it all out, I'll be long gone. Don't you worry, though, I'll take real good care of that girl of yours. Of course, once I take her up to Luna and show her the kind of life she could be living, she might not be *your* girl for much longer."

"She'll never choose you over me!" yelled Shoeshine Boy, hoping with all his heart that he was right about that.

The Man only shrugged. "Maybe, maybe not. Either way, once I've got her off-world, she won't have any way of coming back. Smart girl like that, she'll see it's in her best interest to get real friendly with me real fast."

NEVER SEND A MAN TO DO A MACHINE'S JOB!

Riding the speedrail to the docks to then catch the ferry to the island, Cigarette Girl felt sick. Shoeshine Boy had never called, so she'd been unable to warn him about The Man. She'd phoned Rocket Ray's a few times asking after him, but no one had seen him since early that morning. She was worried now that he'd gone to see The Man, and that something bad might've happened to him.

She knew where she'd find The Man now, though, so she stuck to her plan, reaching the docks just as he was stepping out of a hovercab. Upon seeing her, he tipped his bowler hat and gave her that awful grin of his. She smiled back sweetly, in much the same way she'd smiled at the Mark the day she'd met Shoeshine Boy.

"Sweetheart, you look stunning," said The Man as she approached. "I'm telling you, my restaurateur friend won't know what hit him. The job is yours for sure."

"I sure hope so," she said in an eager pitch. "You have the tickets, right?"

"Got them right here." He patted his jacket where she noticed it bulged a little more than one might expect for two thin tickets, even if you added the bulk of a wallet into the mix.

In the parlance of pickpockets, the object of value one sets their sights on is known as *the poke*. There are a number of ways to retrieve the poke. Often, pickpockets will work with a partner, or *duke man*, to relieve the Mark of his valuables. Cigarette Girl, however, preferred to work alone, and thus had perfected her skills without ever having to rely on anyone else to get her what she was after. And now she knew The Man had in fact brought with him what she was after, and exactly where it was.

"The next ferry should be here soon," The Man said. "We're still a bit early for our launch, but might as well get to the island now and maybe grab a bite to eat before takeoff. Shall we?" He held out his bent arm for her to take, but she pretended not to notice.

"Sure," she told him. "It's just that I haven't been able to reach my boyfriend all day, and I hate the thought of leaving without saying goodbye."

The Man seemed impatient, glancing over to the dock, then back at her. She gave him that smile again—the one that always convinced the customers at the club to choose a nice Cuban hand-rolled over some cheap unfiltered coffin nail.

"Fine, doll. Tell you what, I might as well make a call to my friend up on Luna to let him know to expect us tonight. Why don't you try your beau again while I handle that? Public phones are right over there."

"Oh, thank you!" she told him, and headed toward a set of privacy booths, making sure to swing her hips just so to keep him a little off balance as he followed a few steps behind.

The Man wasn't lying about making a call, just about who he was making it to. While Cigarette Girl took another shot at reaching Shoeshine Boy—this time at their apartment given the time of day—he dialed the number for the authorities and let them know he'd found the thief they were looking for and had locked him in a storage room at an office in the Distillery District.

Once he'd given the police the address and some of the details he'd memorized from the news clipping, The Man ended the call and waited for Cigarette Girl to do the same. A moment later she exited her privacy booth, looking disappointed.

"Still couldn't reach him?" he asked.

"No. I just don't understand what could've happened. This is so unlike him. Maybe I should try him again at the diner."

"Sure, but look, the ferry's arriving now. We don't want to miss it," said The Man, taking her by the arm.

"We can catch the next one," said Cigarette Girl. "You said yourself we have time."

"I think it's best we go now. You can try him again from the island."

"I'd really rather do it now. It'll just take a second."

Cigarette Girl pulled her arm free, but he reached for her again, this time grabbing both her arms, his grip tight enough to bruise.

"You're hurting me," she said. "Let go!"

"I told you, we're leaving now," he insisted.

Cigarette Girl managed to twist free of his grip, then started running, but The Man was in better shoes—ironically, thanks to Shoeshine Boy's fine craftsmanship—and caught up with her easily. He grabbed her again just by the stairs going down to the docks, turning her around so that she swung at him with her free hand, knocking his hat to the floor. Here they struggled for a moment, until she shoved him hard, causing him to lose his balance and fall backward down the concrete steps. Onlookers stood frozen, uncertain as to who they should help.

Cigarette Girl, on the other hand, didn't wait to see if The Man had managed to reach the bottom of the stairs with his neck still intact. Ignoring the strangers' questions, she ran back the way they'd come to where the hovercabs waited. She jumped into the first one she saw that was free and told the driver to step on it. Having seen this very scenario play out in multiple films over his lifetime and considered what he might do if ever he were faced with such a situation, the driver didn't hesitate. It was only once they'd gone a few blocks that Cigarette Girl gave him the address in the Distillery District, hoping that she'd find Shoeshine Boy there, and that she wasn't already too late.

As the hovercab wove its way through traffic, Cigarette Girl opened the bag she'd packed earlier that day. There wasn't much in it besides a few dirty shirts she'd hastily pulled from the hamper to make it look like she'd actually packed, having never intended to go anywhere with The Man. She dug through the soiled clothing a little, her hand finally landing on what she was looking for. The pouch The Man had been carrying inside his jacket.

Here's how the poke had come to be in Cigarette Girl's possession.

She'd of course already noticed the slight bulge under The Man's jacket that, despite his fairly successful attempts to compact it, made his left-side lapel just slightly distorted. Next, she'd made sure his focus was off the poke by distracting him with both her delays and a well-practiced sway of the hips. Then, while in the midst of their struggle by the stairs, Cigarette Girl had made sure to knock his hat off to once more misdirect his attention while simultaneously tugging on his jacket, loosening it just enough in the process for a good look at the poke, and finally for a quick swipe with her nimble fingers as she shoved him down the stairs.

Now came the moment of truth.

Cigarette Girl unzipped the pouch she'd lifted off The Man and looked inside. Just as she'd hoped, it contained the tickets—one with her face on it, the other as yet not activated. *Fool*, she thought. And along with these was whatever money he'd had left over after buying the tickets, which was still a decent amount. There was no time to count it, but at least she could tell from the feel that these bills were legal tender, which was in itself a relief.

She went to close the pouch again, but as she did, she noticed there was also an old-fashioned key inside it. She had no idea what the key was for but imagined that if The Man had brought it with him, it must be important. She zipped it all back up again and returned it to her bag.

Cigarette Girl showed the driver where to pull the hovercab in next to the building so that it was somewhat concealed but still easily accessible, then asked him to wait. Seeing that it was getting late, and he wasn't the type to abandon a woman in the middle of nowhere at any hour, he agreed.

Knowing he wouldn't be returning to his bogus office, The Man hadn't bothered to lock the door behind him, so it was easy for Cigarette Girl to gain access, and as soon as she did, she heard the unmistakable voice of Shoeshine Boy calling for help.

She followed the sound of his voice, running down the hall and up a flight of stairs until she reached the office, surprised to find that this space actually looked well-appointed, and wondered who The Man had swindled to achieve it. But she only wondered this for a split second as her gaze then fell on Shoeshine Boy, who was still locked inside his makeshift prison.

"Oh my goodness!" she said, rushing over to him, seeing that his hands were bloody from his attempts to escape. "Are you alright? What did he do to you?"

"I'm fine," he said. "We just need to figure out a way to get me out of here. Maybe there's something you could use to pry open the gate, since he took the key with him."

Cigarette Girl remembered what she'd found in the pouch, so she dropped her bag to the floor and began rifling through it, finally coming up with the key. It fit the lock perfectly and turned easily, allowing her to open the gate to free him.

The two embraced, then kissed deeply, relieved to be together and that they were both relatively unhurt.

"I'm so sorry I got you involved in all this," Shoeshine Boy said as they pulled apart.

"Never mind that. We need to go," said Cigarette Girl. "I have a car waiting."

Shoeshine Boy nodded, and they turned to run, but just then The Man—looking all the worse for wear from his tumble down the stairs—entered the room. Without hesitating, he went for the desk, reaching under it to grab something he hadn't wanted to risk being caught with as he boarded the rocket.

"Don't even think about running," he said, pointing the gun at them.

Shoeshine Boy immediately moved to stand in front of Cigarette Girl, though he knew the gesture would provide her with only meager protection.

"You know what I want," The Man said. "Give me what you took from me, and we'll call it even. I might even let you walk out of here in one piece."

Even Shoeshine Boy knew better than to take The Man at his word now. Neither he nor Cigarette Girl moved.

"You think I'm joking?" asked The Man. "Kick over that bag of yours, dollface. And don't try anything stupid."

Cigarette Girl slowly raised her arms, and even more slowly moved toward her bag, stretching one of her shapely legs toward it in the hope it'd be enough to buy them some time, maybe even get The Man to drop his guard.

"Nice try," he told her, pointing the gun now squarely at Shoeshine Boy. "You still have a choice, though, gorgeous. It's not too late for you to take your place by my side. Two thieves like us, just think how good we'd be together."

To hear herself compared to him made Cigarette Girl feel sick to her stomach. If they lived through this, she thought to herself, she was going to change her ways, become a better person. Someone more like Shoeshine Boy. Of course, first they had to live through this.

It was as she was thinking this that she heard the police sirens in the distance.

Also hearing the sound, The Man uttered a foul expletive no true gentleman would ever use in front of a lady. He then turned and ran, steps echoing down the stairs, but as he raced outside, he was spotted by the hovercab driver, who used his car to block his path, giving the police just enough time to arrive.

Seeing that The Man still held a gun, the police didn't hesitate. They raised weapons of their own and soon had The Man disarmed and on his knees, handcuffs clicking to an uncomfortably tight lock around his wrists.

Afterward, the police had a lot of questions for Shoeshine Boy and Cigarette Girl, who each told their version of events. Much of her account had come as a surprise to Shoeshine Boy, who until that moment had had no idea how Cigarette Girl had come to meet The Man. But it was the part where she told of how The Man had unwittingly called the cops on himself that had everyone in stitches.

For his part, Shoeshine Boy showed them the newspaper clipping and told them how The Man had planned to frame him. But Shoeshine Boy could easily prove he'd had nothing to do with The Man's previous crimes, as countless people had witnessed him shining shoes on the streets of Toronto for years. Being that he was a decent and likeable man, who often chatted amiably while he worked, Shoeshine Boy could call on any number of customers to vouch for him—not to mention the staff at Rocket Ray's.

The hovercab driver also gave his account of the events since picking up Cigarette Girl, who'd clearly been running from someone quite dangerous.

Satisfied that they had the right guy in cuffs, the police put The Man in their hovercruiser and programmed it to drive him downtown for processing while they checked the office for additional evidence.

"While we're here, maybe we'll come across the shoes," said one of the cops.

"What shoes?" asked Shoeshine Boy.

"Well, this guy robbed a whole lot of people besides you," said the cop. "And one of them happened to get cheated out of a pair of shoes over poker. Turns out the guy with the shoes was an apprentice to some bigshot designer up on Luna, and the shoes—

get this—were one-of-a-kind prototypes for a new line. The designer even offered a reward to get them back."

"How big of a reward?" asked Shoeshine Boy.

His eyes widened as the cop gave him the figure.

"Boy, those people up there are so rich, they'd pay that much just to get a pair of shoes back?" said Cigarette Girl.

Meanwhile, Shoeshine Boy had pulled the drawstring bag off his shoulder and opened it to reveal the pair of shoes that had so badly injured The Man's feet that he'd given them away without a thought.

"Would this be the pair?"

The cop who'd mentioned the reward examined the shoes for a moment.

"Holy cow," he said finally. "These are the shoes. And they still look great, too."

"I cleaned them up a little," said Shoeshine Boy. "As it happens, I know my way around fine footwear too."

"Then you need to get yourself up to Luna," said the cop. "There's a nice reward waiting for you."

Shoeshine Boy smiled at the thought. "Thanks," he told the officer, "but I don't think I'll ever have the means to get up there."

"Actually," said Cigarette Girl. And with that, she reached into her bag and produced the rocket tickets. "There's still one that needs activating. And after all, these belong to us, since they were paid for with our money."

Shoeshine Boy smiled, took the blank ticket, and pressed his thumb to the sensor. An image of his face appeared a moment later.

"There's still time to get you to the launch tonight," said the hovercab driver. "I know a shortcut."

As it happened, after claiming the reward for the shoes, Shoeshine Boy and The Designer got to talking shop. The Designer then told him that since he'd had to fire his old apprentice, he was in the market for a new one, and so it was that Shoeshine Boy got his first job on Luna.

It was in the evenings, when Shoeshine Boy came home from work and Cigarette Girl had yet to start her late shift at the restaurant, that the two of them enjoyed some quiet time together. They would sit by the window wall of their little starter home on the moon and watch the Earth rise above the horizon as the rockets came and went, she sipping from a warm mug of strong coffee that he'd brewed for her, making sure to add plenty of cream, and he from his own cup that more and more resembled her usual.

Things were going well for Shoeshine Boy since he'd started working for The Designer. Having shown what he was capable of, he was quickly moving beyond a mere apprenticeship and had been put to work creating designs of his own. The plan was to continue like this for a time until The Designer was satisfied enough to retire, leaving Shoeshine Boy to run the business while he remained a silent partner. He'd agreed to allow Shoeshine Boy to add his signature stitching to his line of shoes, and was open to allowing him to experiment with other fine leather goods going forward.

For her part, Cigarette Girl was also doing well. A lifetime of having to rely on herself had taught her resourcefulness and imbued her with what she liked to refer to as *moxie*, and so she'd managed to get herself hired on at a fine dining establishment as a hostess—based solely on her previous work experience and qualifications, not on any dubious connections, nor with any implications of some unseemly quid pro quo. True to her promise to herself, she'd given up the life of a pickpocket, and now only practiced her sleight of hand to amuse the restaurant's younger patrons, always ending her demonstrations with a wink and the secret slipping of a lollypop into their pocket to be discovered later.

In the moments when they sat in silence, enjoying the fruits of their shared dreams and labor, they often thought about how far they'd come since meeting at the unassuming location of Rocket Ray's diner in downtown Toronto, and what shape their dreams might take going forward.

"Now that you've given me the moon, what's next?" Cigarette Girl asked one night, a mischievous glint in her eye.

"The moon isn't enough?" asked Shoeshine Boy. "You want the stars too?"

She laughed. "Funny you should mention stars. The restaurant's hosting a special event next month, so I'll be working extra hours to prepare for it. But as a reward for all that extra time, I get to attend the event and also bring a guest."

"That sounds nice."

"Yeah, and you'll never guess, the event is a birthday party for a visiting movie star," she told him. "How would you like to finally get your shot at Lana Monroe?"

Shoeshine Boy's eyes widened. "Are you serious?"

"Sure. I'm not the jealous type. You can come as my plus one and wish her a happy birthday. Finally get your chance to chat up your dream girl."

Shoeshine Boy made a show of thinking it over, then reached out to take her hand. "Nah. I'll come as your guest if you want, but there's only one woman I'd ever consider my dream girl, and she's sitting right here."

He smiled at her then, and Cigarette Girl felt that familiar weakness in the knees before leaning over to plant a great big kiss right on his mouth.

The End

A VIEW LIKE NO OTHER!

The Story Behind
Shoeshine Boy & Cigarette Girl

Warning: Spoilers beyond this point.

For years now, I've had a segment in my newsletter called "The Story Behind the Story" in which each month I choose one of my published works and share inside info with readers. I talk about things like what inspired me to write that particular story, what it means to me, and if there are any fun "easter eggs" in there they might otherwise have missed. So I thought it'd be fun to continue the tradition here, with an exclusive look behind the writing and ultimate publication of *Shoeshine Boy & Cigarette Girl*.

There are many ways to write a story, and each writer has their own process. What's more, that process can change depending on the project. For the most part though, I tend to be what's known as a "discovery writer" or "pantser." What that means is I don't generally do a lot of planning in advance of sitting down to write. I might have an idea about where I want my plot or characters to end up, but most of the details I discover as I go. Often that's how I'll pull together a first draft, later doubling back to reinforce a plot point here or some character development there. Once I know what kind of story I have, that is. Many of my best received stories have started in this way, with me typing away, letting things unfold as if by magic.

When I sat down to write this particular story, all I had was the title. I'd initially decided that I wanted to write a story about a cigarette girl—a job that I saw as a relic of the past that now seems somewhat quaint. Later, I decided to pair her with a shoeshine boy who would become the love of her life. The title came from there, and being simple and lighthearted, kind of brought the tone of the piece built in.

I'd also always wanted to write a story set in Toronto, a city I've known my whole life and lived in for a number of years. I'd started stories set in Toronto many times, but none of these had made it to a complete first draft, let alone publication. For some reason, the city seemed to fit this story perfectly as the meeting place for my protagonists. In retrospect, maybe it has something to do with the fact that my husband and I met while attending college in a suburb of Toronto, and that we started our life together in the heart of this city. How could this story unfold as anything but a love story, when their origin so closely mirrored ours?

Of course this is a piece of fiction, which meant I could have fun with it, so I created an alternate Toronto. One in which I could marry this quirky little love story with elements inspired by the retro-futuristic art and fiction I'd enjoyed as a kid, as well as influence from film noir crime stories I'd encountered in old movies. The end result is a Toronto with familiar landmarks like the iconic CN Tower or the Toronto Islands, but with modifications like the tower serving as a dock for airships, and the islands as launch pads for lunar rockets.

The voice for this story came to me as soon as I began typing. I don't write a lot in omniscient point-of-view, but for some reason this is what this story demanded. There's a certain detachment in it, sure, as a sort of all-knowing entity tells the reader what's happening both within and around the characters. Often, this means the reader knows more than the characters do, and that worked for me. It hearkens back to childhood stories and fairytales that employed this device. And this story has a lot in common with fairytales, if you stop and think about it.

In keeping with the voice and its somewhat removed nature, as well as the title I'd chosen, I decided to keep every character nameless. That is, none of them have proper names, but rather nicknames of a sort. Not giving characters proper names isn't new to me. Taking only protagonists into account for stories both sold and unsold at the time of this writing, I've done this twenty-seven times. But this is the first time I've given my characters descriptors in lieu of names. This worked for me because unlike a randomly-chosen proper name, they immediately evoke an image of who this character is, and how they fit into the story. When you think of a classic cigarette girl, for instance, a certain image comes to mind. In a sense, they're archetypes, and that worked with the kind of story I was trying to tell, and the voice I was using to tell it.

I'm a Latine writer, and the kinds of stories I was raised on, or the kinds of storytellers I came across in my formative years, were often of an oral tradition. Stories that are told in this kind of voice with these kinds of characters. Stories that entertain, but that include lessons if you look beneath the surface. In fact, you'll notice there's a lot about this story that's rooted in my background, as well as in my immigrant story, as you continue to read. While this story is inspired by more than just this, I feel that it honors those traditions, as well as the informal storytellers that I consider some of the greatest influences on my work today. They may not have ever pursued publication or put their tales down on paper, but their words shaped me all the same.

In terms of the characters, I mentioned earlier that I'd previously thought about telling a story that involved a cigarette girl. I grew up during a time when practically every adult (and sadly some disturbingly young kids) smoked. There were smoking sections in restaurants and on airplanes, as if the smoke could somehow be contained. I hated it. I'm asthmatic, and the smoke would irritate my respiratory tract. I still remember the pain in my chest that would remain for hours after I'd spent time in a smoke-filled room. Not to mention the unpleasant stink lingering on my clothing. So I was very happy when Canada cracked down on this and made smoking illegal in common areas. It's for this reason that despite Cigarette Girl's job, I decided to make her a non-smoker. She even dislikes the smoky atmosphere of the club and convinced Shoeshine Boy to quit smoking for his own health. For me, it was important not to make it seem like I thought smoking itself was cool. I was raised on messaging like that and saw the harm it did, and I certainly don't miss it.

I also chose to make Cigarette Girl morally grey, at least in the beginning. She's not exactly a bad person, but because she's had a tough life, she feels justified in stealing, for instance. Because she's been objectified by men her whole life, she feels particularly justified in stealing from them. And, let's face it, she also enjoys her criminal activities. She's good at it so it makes her feel smarter than the Marks. Life has taught her that she can weaponize her sexuality, which gives her a sense of control—something she doesn't have a lot of in other areas of her life. And this works very well for her, until it doesn't. By the end of the story she's become a different person, through her experiences and through her relationship with Shoeshine Boy. This allows her to see that this aspect of her personality no longer serves her, and she makes the decision to change. She has grown, and I think I leave her in a much healthier place from which to start this new facet of her life.

Cigarette Girl isn't my first female thief. One of my early works was also a novelette (albeit cyberpunk) called, "One Last Payday." It's told from the point-of-view of Vega, a woman who also had a rough upbringing and survives by stealing. As with Cigarette Girl, it serves her until it doesn't.

But with Vega, I didn't get quite as detailed into how she commits her crimes. So this time, I spent a lot more of the story outlining the skill involved with pickpocketing. To do that, I looked into the similarities and differences between pickpocketing and the kind of sleight of hand magicians employ. Let me tell you, this is a really fun research rabbit hole to fall into. I learned a good deal more than I included in the story. But don't worry, I'm not about to quit writing to become a small-time criminal.

I knew Cigarette Girl's background would include the fact that she'd learned some of her tricks from a magician, so much of the terminology used in describing the wallet theft when she and Shoeshine Boy first meet, comes from research into that. Later in the story, when she steals the money and tickets from The Man, the explanation is more straight pickpocket terminology. But both involve similar techniques.

This skill, while technically criminal, reveals a lot about who Cigarette Girl is. It's more than just manual dexterity; there's also a good deal of psychology involved in both choosing her Marks and relieving them of their valuables. It gives us clues that, at least in the beginning, she's a survivor at all costs. She's also extremely observant, a quality that serves her well later in the story when she realizes from a casual glance at The Man's shoes, that he's the very same person who conned Shoeshine Boy, and who's been playing her the whole time.

These are qualities she possesses that serve the story. They put her in the places she needs to be and aid her in acting to save herself and help Shoeshine Boy. But it wouldn't be me if I didn't throw in details for my own amusement. For instance, I made Cigarette Girl a sucker for a nice smile. Why? Because *I* am. People I think of as attractive, always have nice smiles. I don't mean a flawless smile, necessarily, just a genuine one that allows their inner joy or goodness to shine through. One of the very first things I noticed about my husband was his smile. And yet, this detail ended up allowing me to shine a light on one key thing: The Man's smile makes Cigarette Girl's skin crawl. That's all we need to know to understand how she feels about him.

So how about Shoeshine Boy? Well, his inclusion in the story came about because I wanted Cigarette Girl to have a love interest; someone also known for an old-fashioned job. Despite the fact that people still shine shoes in Toronto to this day, it's becoming less and less common to see, so this seemed fitting. Shoe shining and repair also play a special part in my life. My parents are of a generation that didn't think of clothing as disposable the way we do now. They grew up mending things, maintaining them, squeezing as much life out of something as they could before declaring it too worn to continue using. As a result, I'd often see my dad shining his shoes, and as a kid I had him teach me how to do it. I don't have occasion to shine shoes as much these days, especially since I tend to live in sneakers, but I'd wager I could still get a mean gloss out of a pair of leather boots if the opportunity arose.

My mom didn't do much shining, herself, but she often got her shoes repaired. She had a "shoe guy" who knew her by name and because they shared a kinship as fellow immigrants, he always went the extra mile so that sometimes we'd pick up her shoes to find they weren't just repaired but improved. I was always impressed by this craft, that seemed like magic to me. As if actual little cobbler elves had done the work. I wanted to honor professionals like this man—this expert in materials, fit, and all things related to beautiful yet functional footwear.

For this reason, I took great care in my research on men's footwear, something I also had a lot of fun with. I even went as far as to include a lengthy segment describing the shoes Shoeshine Boy makes for The Man. But this isn't just a writer saying, "hey, look at all the cool stuff I learned." This passage has a lot to say about who both characters are. We see how much attention to detail Shoeshine Boy puts into his work. How much love and care. And it also reveals that as much as he's proud of his work and thinks the shoes are beautiful, this pales in comparison to how he feels about Cigarette Girl.

By contrast, this same passage reveals how little The Man values things (and by extension, people). He's incapable of seeing either the shoes or Cigarette Girl in the same way Shoeshine Boy does. Their true value is lost on him.

Shoeshine Boy's arc is maybe a touch more subtle than Cigarette Girl's. He's less active, as a protagonist, for one. I like this about them. One thing marginalized authors are often critiqued for when it comes to North American markets and the way Western storytelling traditions work, is that our protagonists aren't active enough. Well, there's a reason for that, beyond differences in storytelling traditions. When you're part of a marginalized community, you don't necessarily have as much agency or control over your environment. You can't always speak up or do much to effect change in the world around you. Depending on your circumstances, you may be completely powerless—for instance if you've experienced life under an oppressive government. So authors that have been marginalized often write their characters into situations in which they may not be able to "save the day" in the classic sense, but they cope or affect their environments in more subtle ways. They're still fighting, but their fight may not be as obvious.

Cigarette Girl is very active. She takes charge of her life as much as she can. When she realizes what The Man has done, she literally fights him. She then rushes to rescue Shoeshine Boy. That's just her personality.

Shoeshine Boy's a little more subdued. He's also less jaded than she is, so he really wants to believe that the people around him are good, and well-intentioned. He wants to give them the benefit of the doubt. He's not naïve per se, he's just got a good heart and tends to project that onto others. But as the story unfolds, he's forced to face the reality that not everyone is as good a person as he is. Unfortunately, by the time he realizes this, it's too late for him to do much in terms of actively changing his circumstances. He goes along with The Man's plan because he feels he has no choice. It says a lot about him that although he does end the story a bit more streetwise than he started out, he doesn't let this knowledge change him. He's still the same good guy, and in that sense has no need to change. That is, after all, why Cigarette Girl loves him, and what prompts her to become better.

The Man may see Shoeshine Boy's inherent goodness as a weakness, but it's actually his greatest strength.

The Man, in this story, represents a kind of person I wish I could tell you was entirely imaginary and not someone I've encountered at many points throughout my life. He's someone who sees goodness, innocence, and desperation, as something to exploit.

When you're an immigrant, it's unfortunately pretty easy to come across people like this. When you're new to a country, you don't automatically know how everything works. There are few, if any, people willing to show you the ropes. You may not even speak the language in order to ask. You're encountering everything others have had a lifetime to learn for the first time. Things they take for granted, are completely...well, *foreign* to you. You're also often starting from scratch in terms of supporting yourself in this new environment. You have to take whatever job might come along—regardless of what your job might've been back home. When you get something half decent going, even if it's not perfect, you're unlikely to complain for fear of rocking the boat and being left with even less, especially if you have a family depending on you. Unfortunately there are people who know this, and who instead of helping, will do what they can to exploit those in this situation.

I immigrated to Canada as an infant, so my experience with people who would take advantage in this way didn't touch me directly in those early years, but I did see it touch my parents. My mom and dad came to Canada with at least some ability to speak English, albeit with strong accents they both have to this day. They are both intelligent, well-read, educated people. Back in Chile they were architects, a career it wasn't possible to continue in quite the same way in Canada because the government would've required that they repeat their training, something they couldn't afford to do back in 1976.

They did eventually end up working in related fields, but initially, they had to take the jobs that came their way. My mom had it particularly rough, performing jobs like working in the Niagara Region's vineyards alongside migrant workers, bent over for hours tying grape vines to wire supports. She also worked for a time as a seamstress. I still recall the days when she couldn't afford daycare and had to take me—then, a toddler—along. In order to keep me quiet so she and the other seamstresses could do their job, I'd be put to work sorting buttons by shape and color. This was something I enjoyed, which is probably why I still recall it decades later.

But during this time, because my parents had accents, some people assumed they were uneducated or even stupid and treated them as such. Some who understood that they weren't stupid, but who still saw how limited they were in their ability to exercise their rights, took advantage of them. My dad recalls being paid far less than his coworkers at one of his early jobs, despite the fact he did as much if not more work than the others. And it wasn't just employers who took advantage. I unfortunately witnessed several such situations while I was growing up.

So it was perhaps inevitable that this story would end up revolving around two good people, working toward simple goals, and the unscrupulous man who would exploit them. Shoeshine Boy in particular represents people like my parents, and others I knew growing up, who had no choice but to take so much crap, simply because they didn't have alternatives. Often, when they were taken advantage of, it would even be presented as if the person were offering them an opportunity they should be grateful for. Remind you of anyone in the story?

I wouldn't say I consciously set out to write this based on those things I witnessed growing up—situations that angered me and made me hyperaware of injustice for the rest of my life. That said, it's probably more than just coincidence that I gave Shoeshine Boy a darker complexion. I'm glad the story turned out this way though, because it rings very true to me, and I'm sure to others who've lived through similar. Fiction always has something to say about our real world, if you dig a little deeper beyond the surface plot.

Aside from being a grifter, The Man is also a misogynist—another type of person I wish I could say I haven't encountered in real life. He notices Cigarette Girl only in the sense that he desires her for her looks and is happy to discard her once those looks fade. He doesn't respect her at all, and assumes she'll fall for his lies, because in his mind "pretty" equals "stupid." He also sees her own desperation to live a different kind of life and thinks he can use that to manipulate her. Everything about him is distasteful. His demeanor, his word choices, and of course the omniscient point-of-view that lets the reader in on what he's thinking.

Now let's go back to discussing the setting. I decided to set this story in an alternate Toronto, but some of the elements are more universal. Specifically, the retro-futuristic elements. I put my characters in a Toronto that blends innovation with the past: there are printed newspapers, paper money, and not a cell phone in sight, but there are also robots, hovercars, and tickets that scan your biometric signature.

This might seem like an unusual choice of setting for a marginalized author. After all, the "retro" part of this harkens back to a period and place that weren't exactly the ideal for those not white, straight, and cisgender. I understand that. My aim isn't to wax nostalgic about the mid-century (or even a little earlier) as if I weren't aware of the disparity. But as I said earlier, this is in many ways, a fairytale. This is the side of retrofuturism that's hopeful and depicts a future we would like to have had—though ideally with much more diversity and inclusivity than we see in older stories and visual art.

A lot of us who grew up on the margins, also grew up watching things like, *The Jetsons*, and wishing our world was a little more like that. We'd watch old footage of the moon landing and imagine a day where we could visit a thriving moon colony—a staple of the genre that I just had to include, especially since it allowed me to play with the idea of "giving your girl the moon." It's that sense of hopefulness I was after.

Shoeshine Boy and Cigarette Girl have one big thing in common right off the bat—they're both dreamers. I wanted to give them a world that inspires their big dreams, and in which it might even be possible to achieve them. This, again, directly stems from my upbringing. My family didn't start out with a lot. We didn't exactly go hungry, but there was little leftover for extras. Many of our belongings came second-hand or were literally made by us. My parents taught me to be resourceful, and to not be wasteful, both qualities that have served me well. Despite our challenging start, they also raised me to be hopeful, and to have faith that if something was meant for you, and you took whatever steps you could take in that direction, things would work out in the end. As with Shoeshine Boy and Cigarette Girl, things didn't come easy, but we never let it take our optimism from us. I wouldn't be living my dream of being a fiction writer if not for that hopeful outlook.

We weren't naïve, mind you. I wouldn't say everyone's dreams can come true without exception, but I will say that what I learned from my family was that the outcome was the least important part. Sometimes, just having a dream, is enough to get you through the rougher parts of life, and that's how it is for these characters for a long time. They have the good fortune that they had a writer looking out for them that wanted them to have a happy ending—and so they get it. But even if they hadn't achieved all their dreams in the end, I like to think they still would've built a good and fulfilling life together, and they still would've grown into better, more complete people, just for knowing each other.

A few final things I threw in just for fun:

The actress Lana Monroe is named for real life stars of the silver screen, Lana Turner and Marilyn Monroe.

The club Cigarette Girl works in is a little nod to Canada geese. I see the geese a lot where I live, usually in pairs, but now and then you see one who has yet to find a life partner. Hence, *The Lone Gander*. It's also a reference to the fact that this is an old school gentleman's club where women aren't allowed, except as staff. Everything about the place is a relic of the past, representative of the kind of thinking that should probably *stay* in the past.

The airships docking at the CN Tower might seem more steampunk than retro-future, but there was a time in our past when airships were very much a part of this idealized future. This detail was directly inspired by the fact that the top of the Empire State Building was originally intended to serve as an airship dock. I simply changed the location and building.

The cabbie who helps Cigarette Girl at the end, is inspired by a real-life hero. When I was in college, a friend and I went out to a downtown Toronto nightclub. When the fun was over, in the wee hours of the morning, we took a bus home. But before we reached our destination, the driver told us he was done for the night and kicked us off. It was late, we weren't dressed for winter weather, and we were two young women alone in the middle of nowhere. We had no choice but to start walking—in heels through a snowstorm.

After a while, a cab drove by and stopped a little way up the street. His light was off, as he was also done for the night, but he'd seen us and was rightly worried we might freeze to death. Even though he'd been heading home, he ended up offering us a ride all the way back to our college dorm. He didn't even charge us for the lift. So the hovercab driver in this story is a tribute to that man, and others like him. Thanks mystery cabbie. You're one of the good ones.

So that's the story about some of the things that went into writing *Shoeshine Boy & Cigarette Girl*. Thing is, once I was done writing—or rather about halfway through—I realized this was a novelette. It was early in 2024. It hadn't been that long since I'd sat at my table at the Nebula Awards Banquet and listened to Curtis C. Chen, that year's presenter for the novelette category, joke about how hard it is to sell a novelette. There are laughingly few markets that will consider this length. Most end up published in single author collections or sent as freebies to newsletter subscribers or patrons, not because they're bad stories, but simply because once you've sent them out to about a half dozen places, if none of them has taken it off your hands, you're out of luck.

If that didn't make things challenging enough, this story didn't just have an awkward length, it was also a mishmash of genres, and most markets tend toward a narrower focus. I knew I had something here, because I'd sent the story to my critique partners—all major award finalists or winners in their own right—and their feedback had told me so, but finding an editor who'd see it the way they did was a whole other matter.

Enter Stars and Sabers.

When I approached Stars and Sabers it was done rather informally. I hadn't planned on reaching out to them, as I knew they published full-length books, or short stories in their anthologies, but I'd never seen them publish a novelette. And yet, I knew that like me, both Gareth L. Powell and Jendia Gammon were fans of all speculative genres. They were about to release their first anthology, a blend of science fiction, fantasy, and horror, to showcase the fact that they were championing all kinds of speculative fiction. So with that in mind, I reached out, told them I had this oddball little story, and asked whether they'd like to take a look at it.

Luckily, Jendia and Gareth fell in love with Shoeshine Boy, Cigarette Girl, and their crazy little adventure and decided to not only take a chance on me and my quirky little story, but to publish it as a standalone book. I knew it had found the perfect home when I saw the excitement with which they approached the project and learned of the plans they had for including art and producing something uniquely special. I saw that they *got* it. That they wanted to see this book succeed as much as I did.

Sometimes things work out that way. Opportunities you didn't even consider, present themselves. To use a quote often attributed to Roman philosopher Seneca, "Luck is what happens when preparation meets opportunity."

In short, a lot of different factors played a part in the journey this story took to publication. A lot of people too, whom I do my best to thank in the acknowledgements. I for one am just glad the quirky little story that insisted I write it has found its way into the real world where I can add it to my bookshelf and now and then maybe take it down to give it another read, just to check that all is still well with my friends.

—P.A. Cornell, Spring 2025

Acknowledgments

I didn't set out to write this book. No, really. It wasn't something I planned. It got its start with a stray thought that cigarette girls used to be a thing, and now aren't, and wouldn't it be interesting to write about one? Then I put that thought aside and moved on, as one does from fleeting thoughts. But one day I just started writing this weird little retro-future story, without really knowing where it was going. I was having fun though, so I kept at it, and even when it was clear it was going to end up being a novelette—a story length that's notoriously difficult to sell—I finished it. I'd grown to love these characters and this alternate world they inhabit.

But I had no idea if what I'd written would resonate with anyone but me.

So I sent the story out to a few trusted first readers, just to get their take on it. Did I have something here, or was I kidding myself?

The first of my readers, as always, was my husband, John-Paul. He found the story charming and only had a few small notes. Always a good sign.

But my husband isn't a writer, so I also sent the story to some author friends, Derrick Boden, Rachael K. Jones, and Jordan Kurella, all not just fantastic writers with award nods and wins under their belts, but also just very cool people. I encourage you to search out and read as much of their work as you can. Trust me, you won't regret it.

These four wonderful people gave me some valuable feedback, as always, and have championed this story from its inception, for which I lack the words to properly thank them, so I hope acknowledging them here counts for something.

As much as they all enjoyed the story and left me feeling like it wasn't just me who saw something worth reading in it, that didn't guarantee I'd find a place to publish it. There are very few venues that accept this length, and the few that do wouldn't necessarily feel this odd little genre blend of a story would fit their vibe.

Which is why I was thrilled that my publishers, Jendia Gammon and Gareth L. Powell, agreed to read it.

Jendia and Gareth started Stars and Sabers Publishing because they love genre. ALL the genres. I thought, if anyone was going to get what I was trying to do with this story, it would be them. Luckily, I was right. I was even more thrilled when they agreed to publish it as a stand-alone book, something that's fairly rare at this length.

I'm also extremely grateful to my editor, Scarlett R. Algee, who ensured every word of this book was doing this story justice. Having worked as an editor myself, I know how much work is involved and how little credit editors often get, so I wanted to ensure I mentioned her here.

The team at Stars and Sabers has been amazing from the start. It's rare you get to work with people that not only like your work but are just as excited to get it to readers as you are. From the earliest days we were sharing ideas for all the things we could do with this story, and how we were going to present it to the world, and I'm thrilled to now see all those dreams become reality.

Special thanks to Kim Herbst, for her amazing cover art and Ahmed Raafat for the incredible vintage-inspired ads included throughout this book. In this age of AI-generated "art" (using the term as loosely as possible) it's a pleasure to get to work with real human artists, especially ones so talented.

In short, the book you hold in your hands is the result of a collaboration between multiple people who love stories, and truly special things happen when such people work together.

In addition, I would like to thank the people in my life who have supported me in my dream to do this thing I love, since I was a little girl. My entire family and extended family, many of whom read my very earliest efforts towards becoming a writer and might even still have a copy or two of the newspaper I hand-wrote and "published" as a kid. My friends, both those who read my work, and those that don't—I love you all regardless. And of course the various communities I'm a part of within the greater writing community: Codex, SFWA, the Odfellows, Alciff Chile, and the Canadian writing community.

Finally, and always, I thank *you*, the readers who give my work their precious time and attention—rare and precious gifts in today's world. Special thanks to those who help spread the word about my stories by word-of-mouth, reviews, and social media shares. This is a tough business to navigate, and your support means the world.

About the Author

P.A. Cornell is an award-winning Chilean-Canadian speculative fiction author. In 2024, she became the first ever Chilean writer to be nominated for the Nebula Award for her story "Once Upon a Time at The Oakmont," also a finalist for the Aurora and World Fantasy Awards. Her fiction has been published in over sixty magazines and anthologies, including four "Best of the Year" anthologies. Her short story "Splits" was the winner of Canada's 2022 Short Works Prize for Published Fiction. That same year she also published her debut science fiction novella, *Lost Cargo*, which was listed as one of the best novellas of 2022 in *Year's Best Canadian Fantasy & Science Fiction, Vol. 1*. Additionally, Cornell has been longlisted for the BSFA Awards for her stories "Things Most Meaningful," "Bright Horizons," and "The Life You've Given Me, Rusty." When not writing, she can be found assembling intricate LEGO builds or drinking ridiculous quantities of tea. Sometimes both. For more on the author and her work, visit her website pacornell.com.

About the Illustrator

Ahmed Raafat is a UK based Egyptian comic book artist.

Ahmed began his career in comics in 2015 with "El-Osba" (Arabic for *The League*), an Egyptian superhero comic book series that he published in Egypt. In 2016 Ahmed moved to the UK, and has since then been working in comics regularly, both mainstream and small press/indie publications.

Ahmed is best known for his work on QUICK STOPS, a comic book anthology series written by director/writer Kevin Smith, inspired by his films, and published by Dark Horse Comics/Secret Stash Press. He has contributed with one issue out of four in Volumes 1 and 3, and was the solo artist for the entire Volume 2. His most recent work is WHO ARE THE POWER PALS, a superhero comedy series also published by Dark Horse comics. He has also previously worked with Netflix and Oni Press.

More from
Stars and Sabers
Publishing

A cross-genre anthology edited by authors and editors Jendia Gammon and Gareth L. Powell featuring short stories from stellar writers of science fiction, fantasy, and horror. This is the debut anthology for Stars and Sabers Publishing. Authors include Adrian Tchaikovsky, Ai Jiang, Alice James, Antony Johnston, Cynthia Pelayo, D.K. Stone, David Quantick, Dennis K. Crosby, Eugen Bacon, Gemma Amor, Greg van Eekhout, Helen Glynn Jones, J.L. Worrad, John Wiswell, Jonathan L. Howard, Kali Wallace, KC Grifant, Khan Wong, Laurel Hightower, Lizbeth Myles, Mya Duong, Paul Cornell, Pedro Iniguez, Peter McLean, Ren Hutchings, Renan Bernardo, Sarah L. Miles, Stark Holborn, and T.L. Huchu.

Publication date Feb. 11, 2025
Paperback: 979-8-9907055-0-0 / Price 19.99
Hardback: 979-8-9907055-1-7 / Price 29.99
Ebook: 979-8-9907055-2-4 / Price 9.99

AN ANTHOLOGY
OF SHADOWS, STARS, AND SABERS
EDITED BY
JENDIA GAMMON AND GARETH L. POWELL

Weaving fantasy and science fiction, Latinx themes, and traditional pulp stylings, this book collects 21 tales of outsiders, explorers, renegades, and dreamers as they navigate the mysteries and perils of the vast sandbox that is the universe.

From magic realism to military science fiction, Lovecraftian cyberpunk yarns, to swashbuckling tales in space, this collection spans the frontiers of the imagination and the vastness of the cosmos.

Publication date July 15, 2025
Paperback: 979-8-9907055-9-3 / Price 19.99
Hardback: 979-8-9914419-1-9 / Price 29.99
Ebook: 979-8-9914419-0-2 / Price 9.99

ECHOES AND EMBERS
SPECULATIVE STORIES
PEDRO INIGUEZ
Bram Stoker Award Winner

Of Enchantment, Enigma, and the Infinite is an anthology with magical themes edited by Jendia Gammon and Gareth L. Powell, featuring fantastical short stories from masters of speculative fiction.

Contributing authors include:

Ai Jiang, Alice James, Angela Sylvaine, Anne Corlett, Chris Panatier, Cynthia Pelayo, D.K. Stone, Dana Gricken, David Quantick, Dennis K. Crosby, Eddie Robson, Eliane Boey, Eugen Bacon, Guido Eekhaut, Helen Glynn Jones, Ian Green, J.L. Worrad, James Bennett, Jenny Rae Rappaport, Jonathan Maberry, Kali Wallace, KC Grifant, Khan Wong, Lili Hayward, Lizbeth Myles, Mya Duong, P.A. Cornell, Ren Hutchings, Renan Bernardo, Sarah L. Miles, and Somto Ihezue.

Publication date Aug. 5, 2025
Paperback: 979-8-9907055-3-1 / Price 19.99
Hardback: 979-8-9907055-4-8 / Price 29.99
Ebook: 979-8-9907055-5-5 / Price 9.99

AN ANTHOLOGY
OF ENCHANTMENT, ENIGMA, AND THE INFINITE
EDITED BY
JENDIA GAMMON AND GARETH L. POWELL

When a precocious Guardian in Sector Z in New Inku'lulu—an elite space outpost—misuses her sound magic, the Guardians punish her by stripping away her magical ability.

Now Chant'L is exiled to Savage Mound, a sound island on planet Wiimb-ó, and grows increasingly vengeful—until she discovers that magic is inborn, never truly lost or taken. She channels energy from two spirit moons and reclaims her sound magic.

Chant'L summons the Nga'phandileh, creatures of unreality. But her magic is more than she bargained for when an uncontained trinity of the hive mind slips from unreality and brings peril to the federation of planets.

Now the Guardians in Sector Z find themselves with a massive catastrophe they must not only keep secret, but resolve.

A science fiction horror from an award-winning queen of Afro-Irreal genre bending.

A glossary of Bantu, Afrocentric and authorly-crafted words complements this genre-bending, cross-cultural novella. Something beautiful, something dark in lyrical language packed with affection, dread, anguish and hope.

Publication date September 2, 2025
Paperback: 979-8-9914419-2-6 / Price 13.99
Hardback: 979-8-9914419-4-0 / Price 19.99
Ebook: 979-8-9914419-3-3 / Price 5.99

THE
NGA'PHANDILEH
WHISPERER
A SAUÚTIVERSE NOVELLA
Eugen Bacon
Solstice, British Fantasy Award Winner & Otherwise Fellow

Stacey Kells never expected to fall out of reality when she packed her bags, got into a camper van with her two brothers and their best friend, and started travelling west. Sure, they might have said something like that—that's kind of the point of going off the grid, isn't it? But no one thought it would happen quite so literally. Then the world got real empty, and it stayed empty.

Now it's just the four of them, and a map that doesn't make sense, and miles upon miles of desert and sky and endless empty highway. They embarked on this road trip to figure out what to do with their lives—but their lives don't seem to exist anymore, and there may not be a way back home.

The Legend Liminal is a story about grief and hope, and the way we find lifelines in each other when we can't break free of the spiral of the past.

Publication date September 30, 2025
Paperback: 979-8-9914419-5-7 / Price 13.99
Ebook: 979-8-9914419-6-4 / Price 5.99

THE
LEGEND
LIMINAL
REN HUTCHINGS

9 798989 914419